TARRADIL

OFF BEAT TALES AND ALCHEMICAL EATS

WENDY SPENCELEY

Tarradiddle - Offbeat Tales and Alchemical Eats

By Wendy Spenceley

Copyright © 2011 Wendy Spenceley

Blog: offbeattales.wordpress.com

THIS BOOK IS DEDICATED WITH LOVE AND
RESPECT TO

The Moon

CONTENTS

INTRODUCTION

If you have bought this book, you may have purchased it as a present for someone or for yourself. I very seldom read the introduction of a book because I'm usually too excited and want to get onto the story straight away. So, if you are reading this, then thank you for the extra time. I've purposely included this introduction to enlighten those who seek to find truth and transformation in everything they do.

To explain, the book has two layers. On one level it is a book of short stories and poetry with some special recipes that you can read and cook with yourself and/or share with friends. However, on another level it is a work of Transformational Alchemy that will enhance and complement your soul if you choose to include this powerful practice in your recipes.

So here you have some stories to read and some great recipes to experiment with and I hope they enable you to discover your own Alchemy. If you do like to take things a little further, have a look at the Alchemical Symbols at the start of each section.

Before you start your meal, be it alone or with friends, close your eyes and take 12 deep breaths in and out, then open your eyes and look at the Alchemical Symbols for a few minutes. Close your eyes again and notice any thoughts that come to you as they may be important for you (or for those around you) and what you are about to experience while you incorporate Transformational Alchemy into your creative pursuits. When you have done this take a couple of deep breaths and continue with your evening.

You will see also, some words at the beginning of each chapter in quotation marks. They relate to Life Symbols that appear in the e-book edition of this book (see also footnote on Life Symbols*). I traced them over the dishes (2 inches above) when I brought them to fruition because I believe they give that extra Transformational ingredient to the recipes.

If you see a word that appears to be negative to you, please don't be put off, often one has to work through a negative process to find balance and feel light again (see boxes at the end of each recipe for more insight). Do feel free to use your own system to incorporate Transformational Alchemy into the recipes - not everything is set in stone. Also not everything is constant in any metaphysical activity.

There are lots of books on the market to enable you to tap into your own creativity. I can recommend the author and mentor, Tom Evans (** see footnote).

Another quite simple, yet powerful, symbol I use regularly is a heart which is why I have included a picture of a heart at the end of the book. You may like to imagine the heart floating over or in any of the recipes, or even bring it into your meditation practice. I use the heart symbol because I feel it represents Unconditional Love in its purest sense. It brings a light Alchemical balance to all that we do and in turn, ripples outwards to all of life on this earth and, potentially, to other planets.

If you'd like to incorporate the five elements of Earth, Wind, Fire, Water and Air into your cookery, I would suggest that the 5 pointed star, encased in a circle, known as a pentacle, may lead you to a kind of metaphysical completion (see also the back of this book for an illustration).

Enjoy the prose, eat well and harness your own Alchemy.

Wendy

PS: You can also visit my Blog: offbeattales.wordpress.com

* Life Symbols have been included with the kind permission of Kay Kraty – if you wish to know more about the Life Symbols please contact Kay at KayKraty@aol.com

** I would like to recommend Flavours of Thought – Recipes for Fresh Thinking by Tom Evans and his other books. You can contact Tom at www.tomevans.co and www.tomevans.co/witwtm/

BEGINNINGS

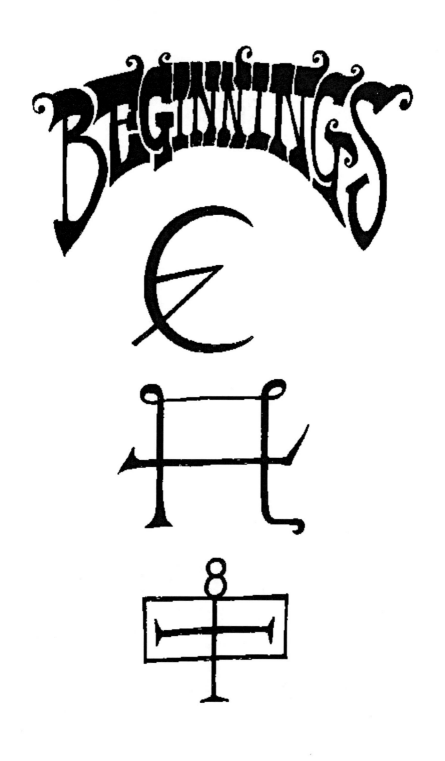

SPRING

MIX

WORLD OF SPIRIT

THE FEATHERED COLLECTOR

Carly put her foot down further on the accelerator as Gus dug his nails into the fabric of the seat of the MG. His voice slowed to a muffle; a dubbed out bass as she sped along the curved lanes of suburbia, towards the city.

His words entered her thoughts at intervals as the downward slopes made her ears pop. Gus kept talking and talking, jumping from subject to subject. Everything about her was wrong for him, apparently; he liked to entertain, she didn't. He preferred her dressed smartly in a suit; the kind she might choose for his mother. Yet she liked the floating fabrics and intricacy of bright Buddhist colours. The kind that felt comfortable and sensual on her skin.

Gus's job was as demanding as his personality and his friends insisted on drink fuelled parties where the entertaining was cold and competitive. There was no warmth or friendliness in these people. It hadn't always been like this, where had he gone, or was it she who was gone? There was no relating in their relationship just a rigorous routine where she was compelled to focus on Gus, his life and his work.

A thud broke her thoughts and caused her head to jolt backwards. Something hit the wind-screen, something big and bird-like!

"What was that?" said Gus in a flimsy and not really interested voice.

"Wait here." Carly stepped out of the car and the twins stirred in their seats.

As she walked round to the front of the car and saw it lying there Gus levered himself out of the passenger side and lit a cigarette.

"Look Gus, an Owl! What a beautiful thing, come here and help me." Carly pulled off her cardigan and wrapped it around the creature.

"Is it dead then?" he sneered through an extension of thick smoke.

"Come on Gus, put that thing out will you? It's still alive. Let's do something please. Let's help it!"

"Gimme a break Carls, I got a 6am start. It's already eight; leave it for Christ's sake. Can we get back, huh? Come on love, get in the car?"

"No, I won't. Look Gus, we can do something here. It's just the wing, look at its great eyes."

The creature looked up at Carly. Orange eyes opened and closed. With each of its tiny breaths came a growing sense of panic in her for its life. It was the kind of panic that irritated her soul.

Carly lifted her head gently and watched Gus walk away towards a field of yellow rape crop. The cigarette smoke curled upwards from his head in dark dirty circles as he leant dejectedly on a fence.

"Let's go Carly; I haven't got time for this."

It was the emphasis on the word time that did it, like the knife that seared across her breast during her last operation. "I don't have time" she voiced this to herself. Neither did the Owl, there was no time for either of them.

Gently and quickly, she scooped up the great bird and dropped it softly onto the passenger seat. As she ran around to the front of the car, her mules twisted on the gravel. A searing pain shot up her ankle causing her to limp awkwardly.

Luckily the engine was warm and the sports car started first turn. It made a noise akin to the screech of a wounded heron. With all her strength, she spun the car round onto the opposite side of the road and in anger Gus lunged to hit the small boot with his palm. Missing the car, he stumbled onto the gravel and let out a pathetic whimper. Carly observed this spectacle through the mirror as he rolled awkwardly onto the pavement, like a spoilt child crawling towards a tired parent.

She was now travelling in the opposite direction to the City and the twins had woken up; they quietly entertained each other. Why on earth didn't they have a practical car? Still now they were free she breathed out the years of repressed anger and turned to take a look at the Owl;

"Please be ok."

"What is it Mummy" Ella was now inquisitive from the back.

"It's an Owl sweetheart and she's not very well."

"Why?"

"She flew into the car."
"Where's Daddy" ventured Vicky. That's a point, she hadn't thought of the twins or what to say to them. She felt the inevitable tears prickle at her eyes.

"Don't worry darling, Daddy will be fine and you know how he likes to walk. We'll see him again soon" she lied.

"Where are we going?" Ella again.

"We'll take him to the Owl hospital darling. It's called the Vet."

"OK." Ella sank quietly back into her chair.

The twins were smart for their 4 years of age and she hadn't thought about what to say to them. She had just fled, knowing that this was her chance to do something about all the mess he had caused them. The twins were terrified of Gus and she'd seen their look, like the one the Owl was giving her now. Its eyes were bright and fearful and everything she felt was reflected in them. To her, at this point in time, everything was so frighteningly wrong!

Luckily the twins were tired and fell into a deep sleep to the sound of the engine. Soon, Carly came to a local town they'd stopped at previously and carefully she wound her way up the High Street. Eventually they stopped alongside the first person they came across and she lowered the window;

"I've hit an owl" the stranger wore a hoodie and it dawned on her how crazy she must have sounded and aged, so aged for her 30 years.

"Wow, that's neat."

"No it's not neat! Please, tell me where the vet is."

"Easy, vet's about 200 yards down there on your left. He'll be shut now though. Lives above with his Mrs., they won't answer you."

"Let's see shall we?" Off she went again and seconds later she was parking up in front of an old white building.

The twins were still asleep so she left them to it, making sure they were within earshot. Carly gently lifted her new friend from the passenger seat.

"Come on sweetheart let's get you sorted out."

Feathers twitched in her hands as she carried her Owl towards the door. Her Owl! It's a wild animal. What was she thinking! She rang the doorbell, keeping her finger pressed on it until an older woman appeared at the window;

"Take your hand off the bell will you! And anyway, what do you want?"

"Help me please. I've got this Owl, my children are asleep in the car and we need help."

"Kids in a car like that? That's what I mean; stupid!"

"Never mind that, help me please, it's hurt." Carly held up the Owl, desperate to get this person to notice what was going on.
"Wait a minute, that's David's Owl! How did you get it?"

"I hit it with the car. Can you help me or not!"

"No we're an equine vet, you need to take it to David. He tamed it himself, I know that much and he's very attached to that one too. Just wait here; I write down directions."

The woman moved away from the window so Carly put the Owl back on its seat;

"Hold on my love. I'll get you home, not long now."

Her heart was banging in her throat causing waves of nausea. What if she died, what if this poor man's Owl couldn't hold out. The window flew open again;

"Here catch this; they're directions to David Faraday's house. You can't miss it, the Aviaries are huge and you'll see them from the lane."

"Thank you so much."

"You're welcome and, well, drive carefully OK?"

Carly waved a goodbye, fell back into the driver's seat and placed the Owl back in the place next to her. She needed to hurry but felt exhausted. Panicking now, she pressed the directions to the steering wheel to study them carefully. Dangerously she drove with her thoughts racing along to the tune of the engine. Oh, what had she done! She looked down at the Owl and spoke to it thinking that somehow this might encourage it to stay alive.

"Thank you beautiful bird. Thank you for saving us but, what do I do now?"
Its eyes opened and closed heavily again. Why was she dithering, it really didn't matter about her, and the girls were ok right now;

"I hope I can save you."

Eventually she reached a right fork in the road and winced as the wire wheels smashed down into deep wet pot holes. Gus's affair 5 years ago was ridiculous. She tried to forgive him but she certainly could not forget it. It was a cliché that she came to detest while he became more aggressive and difficult.

Finally the car slowed to a stop as she realised the antique MG BGT was probably the only security she would retain from the breakup. Breakup, what would she say to her family? She'd really done it now, it was happening, and when she least expected anything to happen. What next? What about the twins?

Again, she lifted her precious creature from the car, the Owl should be her focus not her and anyway it wasn't "her" creature. It belonged to this David Faraday fellow, if anyone. What was he going to think of her? Nothing of course! Her thoughts raced like ants over a sticky pot of jam. He would think nothing because he would be worried, worried about his Owl.

She looked up as the door to the old house opened. A man with long dark hair bunched back into a colourful band approached her. He spoke to her with a gentle voice that calmed her thoughts immediately. Carefully, he lifted the owl from her arms;

"I'm sorry – she just flew.. I, well.. I'm, so sorry..." Tears slid quickly down her cheeks, still hot as they reached her exposed neck.

"I know. Don't worry, it's nothing."

He looked into her eyes with a gaze that brushed sensually across her heart.

"Come now, you have children yes? Bring them inside. I have spare rooms?"

"What, I couldn't.. I... How do you know they are with me?"

They both looked down at the Owl.

"Don't worry, she's a special Owl, you realise? I asked her to bring you to me."

"What do you mean?"

"Just thank her with your heart, if you'd like to of course?"

"I would yes, but look at her. Isn't she badly hurt and all because of me!"

"She'll be fine. Come now it's cold, you need sleep and I must fix her wing. It's easy enough then we'll take a look at that ankle, OK?"

"But I can't, I've caused you enough trouble already."

"Stay here tonight at least, please. You'll know what you need to do by the morning.

" LOYALTY / DEVOTION "

OWL FACED SESAME MUSHROOMS

No Owls have been harmed making this lovely fungi!

6 Large Flat Field Mushrooms

12 Slices of Cucumber

1 Large Onion (peeled and chopped finely)

3 Cloves Garlic (peeled and chopped)

1 Inch Cube of Fresh Ginger (peeled and chopped)

5 Tablespoons of Vegetable Oil

2 Teaspoons of Tomato Puree (mixed up with 2

tablespoons of water)

Pinch of Cayenne Pepper

1 Teaspoon of Ground Cumin

2 Teaspoons of Ground Coriander

Pinch of Ground Black Pepper

1 tablespoon of Lemon Juice

1 tablespoon Sesame Seeds (roasted)

For Presentation:

1 Lettuce

2 Lemons cut into Quarters

Pre-heat oven to 180°C / 350° / Gas Mark 4.

Gently remove the mushroom stalks but don't throw them away. Wash the mushrooms and the stalks and put them to one side.

Fry the onions, garlic and ginger in a saucepan with the vegetable oil then add the rest of the ingredients (except for the cucumber slices). Mix well and bring to the boil.

Heat some oil in a non stick frying pan and add the mushrooms and the stalks so that they brown off. Remove from heat and place the stalks to one side. Place the mushroom tops (undersides facing upwards) onto a greased baking tray.

Put the curry sauce onto each mushroom then use the cucumber slices for eyes and the mushroom stalks for the beak. Bake in the oven for 30 mins and serve on a bed of lettuce with a quarter of lemon.

For Alchemical Transformation
"CHALLENGE / OPPORTUNITY" resonates to the frequency of number 43; the numerology of which: Builds from the original plan. Allows the old order to dissolve, so a new self can emerge.
"LOYALTY / DEVOTION" resonates to the frequency of number 158; the numerology of which is: Uplifted through beauty. Can get caught in a stubborn insistence, but need to accept the reality of change.
PROCESS THE ABOVE WHILE PREPARING THE DISH

" IGNORANCE / BLISS "

QUAKER HOUSE

Carefully I open the door to a new world of unknown faith. The room is cool after the heat of autumn sun outside and I quietly remove my sandals. Silence flows over my body. I wish my Mother had been more approachable. I need to know more about my Father who left us 30 years ago.

A breath sounds itself into the room as a warm individual walks towards me with relaxed shoulders and a whimsical smile.

"Come quietly" he whispers, "we sit in silence" and he beckons me towards an armchair placed close to the other town folk who sit gently in an individual, yet collective peace.

I came here to encounter some calm and slowly, I lapse into an old meditation technique, not quite fitting with the mood of this gentle space. I try to focus. What can I do now that I'm feeling at a loss with myself. How do I join these new friends on their journey, become part of their world? I look secretively around the room from Quaker to Quaker as they rest in silence.

I start to carefully pick out individuals for my latest fiction searching around the room to see interesting beings whose eyes are closed, taking in the silence.

In row 3 a lady of retirement age wears a purple suit and a beret to match. She sits straight, smartly dressed and tidily made up. I watch her posture; her hands are crossed inwards on her lap and she sits serenely and in confidence. I contemplate her life and how she may have arrived here today and notice how she holds her stature. Yet there is frailness brought on by her age and despite this, I imagine her to be open and sociable. I will call her Lady Chartres.

Now in row 5, sits a thirty something man in lose faded jeans, an oversized shirt and a wooden necklace. I name him Michael; his limbs are open and he is trouble free. I decide he writes lyrics for a band. In his head he contemplates sounds and words merging together. It is calmness that he finds at these meetings that facilitates his imagination.

I move my head slightly to see an older gent - still with a weathered face and a furrowed brow. Just as I start to mentally work him into a character for chapter 2, his eyes flicker open! Eyes of sea blue are shining brightly and directly into mine. His body quickly unfolds. Immediately, I can feel my heart leaping. This shy looking man is about to break the Quaker silence. He opens his mouth to speak;

"I'd like to say good morning to my daughter who joins us today for the first time. I'd like to say, for the first time, good morning to my daughter....!"

He stares directly at me and smiles, whereupon I freeze.

" DOUBT "

DADDY ELF'S HERB AND GOATS CHEESE SALAD

1 Organic Lettuce of your choice (chopped)

4 Spring Onions (chopped)

1 Handful of Rocket (chopped)

1 Handful of Marjoram (chopped)

1 Handful Basil (chopped)

1 Handful of Cranberries

1 Handful Pine Nuts Roasted

1 Packet of Solid Goats Cheese chopped into cubes

For Dressing:

Splash of Oil

Splash of White Wine

Splash of Balsamic Vinegar

6 Seeded Baps - halved and buttered

To roast the nuts, preheat the oven to 160°C / 325°F / Gas Mark 3. Place the nuts on a baking sheets and bake for 10 mins while you make the rest of the salad.

Place all the other ingredients into a large salad bowl – roughly chopped then mix in the roasted nuts.

Put all the ingredients into a jug. Beat with a fork. Divide into bowls and add a seeded bap to serve.

For Alchemical Transformation

"IGNORANCE / BLISS" resonates to the frequency of number 131; the numerology of which is: Inspired by the blueprint to know 'no-thing'. Allows the mind to be silent and touch the void.

"DOUBT" resonates to the frequency of number 80; the numerology of which: Moves away from personality issues in order to get on with the spiritual task. Accepts the job of co-creator.

PROCESS THE ABOVE WHILE PREPARING THE DISH

" ADDICTION / HABIT "

TOAST

I stand in the gallery rigid, watching over the residents while they eat. It is the evening meal and she is gently taking bites from a triangle of toast. It's all she wants at this time of day, all she eats and all she needs or so she tells me;

"It's the warm comfort of a little melted butter on a scorched piece of bread Karl".

The pleasure is revealing itself now on her smooth oval face as it did the day before when we ate together.

Each afternoon since her arrival I have watched, worked and walked with her. Abbie commands far too much of my attention and my colleagues raise eyebrows when I discuss her progress. I'm anxious that my time as her assigned analyst is perhaps in jeopardy, while I become more and more important to her. Or, is it really that she's important to me? Together we've managed to break the hold of the anorexia gripping her very being. I don't know why but more and more each day she appears to be happier.

It was probably clear I wasn't watching the residents properly as I mulled over how the patient-doctor relationship had become blurred. The ties of dependency have slowly tightened on both our parts. Soon the professional rules will kick in and I will have to let her go; face the fact that I will remain alone and broken for the rest of my time here.

I stand silent, stiff and professional as I watch her. She, well she is as timid as a selfless animal, and so grateful for my support.

"She's eating now Karl."

Thomas, my older colleague, places a reassuring hand on my shoulder as he speaks. He mentored me through my medical studies, was a counsellor when my father died and a friend through my divorce.

"How did you know?" I respond.

"Know what?"

"Don't play with me Thomas, I know you can see it and I know you know this is not a healthy scenario for the Trust". I was impatient with my senior and resented him for pretending not to read my thoughts.

"Ah, so you are watching her then?"

I sighed "Yes Thomas, I watch her because what else can I do? Does anyone else watch her; you know; really take time and admit she is well? It is all I feel I can do, just care.

"Yes, I see" was his quiet response.

"She is so beautiful, look at her Thomas. Look at the way she eats now. She trusts me! Yet you know in her company, I am the fragile one. At any moment she could regress and we'll all be compromised."

"If I didn't know she needed you Karl, I might have her removed? You know transferred so to speak?"

"Hell Thomas, what are you saying? Are you're asking me to make that decision now? You know I can't do that, I just won't. You do it! You're the Professional-in-Charge!"

"Look Karl, I spoke with Sir Arnold Day, her Father, last week? You know him don't you?"

"Arnold Day? Yes I know him, I had no idea he was her Father though? I knew him at Cambridge but wait; he's a pharmaceutical tycoon, is he not? So anyway, what were you saying?"

"I told him about the progress you've made with Abbie and well, to my mind, he was a little too quick to extend his gratefulness. He was so grateful in fact, that my suggestion that he visit her occasionally fell sadly upon deaf ears. For some reason, he seems very ashamed, embarrassed about her almost. He was rather keen to be sure she could stay here!"

"And?"

"Well, the following day Arnold Day Pharmaceuticals credited our Trust account with £50,000. Karl, it's apparent that your "project" is somewhat alone in this world."

Through all this awkward conversing my stare did not move from her small frame. I followed the gaze of her green eyes through the window where two hares boxed on the lawn. The movement of their paws mirrored the pounding in my chest and my spirit would not, and could not, leave her.

"I'm taking her Thomas, she'll live with me."

The statement fell from my lips like a delicate glass fountain, then came the quiet response from my colleague;

"When?"

"I'll send the car this Friday. She does not belong here."

"Very well Karl, Friday it is."

Thomas's heavy hand left my shoulder and I continued my gaze. His footsteps faded as he departed. Had he understood?

HAPPY HERRING TOASTIES

3 Large Smoked Herrings (preferably Baltic and with
heads and skins removed)
100ml Crème Fraiche
100g Cottage Cheese
1 Pickled Gherkin

To Serve

Loaf of seedy bread and butter (optional)
Sprig of Watercress to serve

Cut the fish into small pieces and chop the gherkin.

Mix together crème fraiche and cottage cheese then
add the chopped fish and gherkin.

Toast the bread and spread the mixture generously
over the top with a sprig of watercress to serve.

Serves 3-4

For Alchemical Transformation

"ADDICTION / HABIT" resonates to the frequency of number 6; the numerology of which is: Devotion to the cause. Caught up in the idealism of perfection, which requires 'dying' to illusion in order to follow truth.

"BALANCING FEMININE ENERGY" resonates to the frequency of number 31; the numerology of which: Makes ideas visible. Sees what is needed and enables it to happen. Births the new.

PROCESS THE ABOVE WHILE PREPARING THE DISH

RECEIVER

SOLVE

SON

BEWARE OF ORANGE COLOURED VEG

Jilly kissed her husband goodbye as he stiffened and admired himself in front of the mirror. Husband! How did *that* happen she wondered as he shrugged her off and headed for the door.

Why had she agreed to marry him? Her Father, a pushy man had always wanted a son to pass the family business to. Yet when it came to family, her Father was as cold as this man he'd employed. Sadly, Jilly's Father used people and only acknowledged her when he had decided to impress this wet fish of a man upon her.

Jilly regarded her husband's back as he opened the door, and she realised her mistake. Tom's only concern was the family business and since their quick marriage he hardly noticed her. He responded only to her Father's feeble whims.

"See you later then." The door slammed shut and the aged glass shook the doorframe behind him leaving a searing sound in her ears.

"Pumpkin Tali" she complained to the black cat following her back into the kitchen.

"He wants roast pumpkin and walnuts for dinner. Who cares if it's damn well Halloween!" Talison meowed and jumped up onto the stool next to her, flashing his rice green eyes.

"I love you Tali." She softened and stroked her fingers along the spine of her feline who purred affectionately.

"Yes, it's you I love Tali, not him – what an idiot!"
She made a decision not to give into the negative thought patterns. Breathing deeply she focused herself and resolved to channel this overwhelming knife-edged energy into chopping a large Pumpkin;

"It's good to prepare ahead Tali. We'll sleep this afternoon."

It was huge, a hard rotund ball of orange. She plunged the knife into the top and found it really difficult to cut around the remains of the stalk. As she did so Tali distracted her with a loud meow.

"What's wrong Tali? What.. Ouch!" The knife slipped and the blade sliced into her finger. Blood oozed from the wound like sticky red treacle.

"Tali you mad animal, can't you behave?"

The pumpkin, complete with knife, fell to the floor. Jilly's head spun and her knees buckled underneath her. The sounds outside became muffled and all she saw were black and silver spots. Unable to save herself, Jilly fell backwards. Her head hit the kitchen cabinet. A faint sound of paws landed on the stone floor beside her while the noise from outside faded to a whisper. Jilly felt the brush of Tali's fur on her arm and she lost consciousness.

"Come on girl, bring yourself round. Hey girl!" snapped an angry voice. Jilly felt nauseous.

"Jilly, my name's Jilly."

"What's that girl?

"Jilly Stobbard, 286 Lovelace Road, Surbiton."

"C'mon, sit up. Drink!"

"Where am I? Who are you?"

"Drink, here, drink this."

A short blue face starred at her harshly then thrust a purple glass bottle towards her mouth.

"Oh come on, we haven't got all day, if you want to get rid of him."

Jilly passed out again. The sight of a person with a blue face and a tall black hat was just too much. She heard the mumbling of annoyed female voices and forceful hands bundled her dead weight onto an uncomfortable makeshift stretcher.

"OK, get her to the middle. We've got to get this potion made while we still have the full moon, and we need her to do it."   Jilly drifted in and out of consciousness with the movement of the bouncing stretcher.

The next thing she knew, she was upright in an armchair made of twisted Willow. She slowly opened her eyes to the sounds of concerned voices.
"Here she comes, she's back."
"What's your name again girl?" said the older of the strange looking women.

"Jilly, I told you, I'm Jilly Stobbard and who on earth are you?"

Jilly looked around the circular room. It was fleshy and orange, a bright, orange. Where was she?

"Ha ha! Listen to that sisters, 'Who on earth' she's asking us!"

Jilly was annoyed at these small but irritating women who all seemed to be laughing at her misfortune. At the same time, she did notice her finger had been expertly bandaged.

"Tell me what's going on?"
"OK, alright, be calm. I'm Isate, and these are the Sisters of the Pumpkin."

"What?"
"The Pumpkin Witches, we live here. You called on us, remember? Something about a trouble-some husband? Want to get rid of him, don't you?"

"Yes but..."

"No buts, you're here now and we can sort it. We need you though, we need your blood. Have a look, nice and thick eh?" A bottle of sticky red stuff waved chaotically under Jilly's nose.

She felt dizzy again as she watched Isate, who appeared to be the leader of the group, lift the bottle of sanguine coloured liquid into the air to examine it.

"Splendid, splendid, good blood you have Jilly. Leave it to us to complete the tincture and all will be ready and well. You just sit there and eat some pumpkin, it's good for you."

A blue faced disciple appeared at Isate's command and handed Jilly a plate of roast pumpkin. She pushed it away;

"I'm not eating that! Look, are you saying you want to poison my husband?!"

"Of course, of course, you don't need all that nonsense he brings you. Come now, relax."

Isate tipped the thick red liquid into a cauldron of bubbling liquid. The fumes wafted across the room and clung to the inside of Jilly's nostrils. A metallically smell accentuated the rising nausea.

"Isate, please, this is... Well I mean it's not really necessary or legal, surely! I mean he's a bit of a slime but you can't, I mean what will you do? You can't poison him? I don't think I want that. I..."

Before she could say anything further, one of the blue faced sisters grabbed her nose and forced her head back. The only way she could continue to breathe was to open her mouth. In went a spoonful of the orange pumpkin. She choked it back, struggling to breath.

"Better dear?" smiled the devious assistant.

"Delicious, thank you." Jilly felt the evil in her rising, Isate's idea now appealed to her immensely. The magical pumpkin pulp was warming her stomach, altering her mental state of being.

"Good, good" beamed Isate.

"Here Elfina, take the broom stick and put 12 drops of this in his whisky. Now go! Fly sister!"

There was a rush of warm air as Elfina expertly lifted the broom into the air and swiftly left the centre of the pumpkin, through an orange tunnel.

Jilly then found herself joining the circle of Witches as they chanted their deadly words. She loved it. Brilliant. Just brilliant! The self centred creep would be soon be chocking on their poison. Arm in arm the Witches circle-dance grew faster and faster. Jilly became dizzier and dizzier and the link of their arms became tighter. She closed her eyes and the chanting began to fade.

After a few minutes of quietness the chants were replaced by voices talking over her. Jilly was lying down now with lights blurring brightly above. She slowly made out concerned faces and white coats.

"Is she OK Dr?" It was the nurse who spoke first. "Can we let them in now?"

"Jilly. Talk to me, please? I'm Dr Thomas, can you hear me?"

Once again, she felt herself regaining full consciousness.

"Err, yes err. Dr Thomas you say?"

"Yes Jilly good, Here you go, sit yourself up OK? That's right, have a pillow now."

"Dr Thomas, please could you ring my husband, I need to speak to him."

"Husband? Yes, well Jilly. I have some people here who'd like to talk to you about your husband."

Jilly turned her head away from the Doctor. The door of the white hospital room opened and two police officers entered.

"Good morning Jilly. We'd like to have a few words with you about Mr Stobbard's current condition..."

" MYSTERY "

ROASTED PUMPKIN PERFECTION

1 Small Pumpkin (chopped into cubes)
250g Roquefort Cheese
100g Walnuts
Olive Oil or Corn Oil
Packet of fresh Rosemary

Pre-heat your oven to 180°C / 375°F / Gas Mark 5 and Oil a ceramic plate or roasting tin with the oil of your choice.

Chop the Roquefort into chunks and place evenly over the pumpkin pieces. Do the same with the walnuts and sprinkle over a little more oil before topping off with the sprigs of Rosemary.

Place in the middle of the oven for 40 minutes.
Serves 4

For Alchemical Transformation

"GUIDANCE / TEACHING" resonates to the frequency of number 116; the numerology of which: Gives love to the smallest of movements. The rhythm of action and reaction infused with spirit.

"MYSTERY" resonates to the frequency of number 175; the numerology of which: Works with the systems beyond human understanding. Rises up to the divine.

PROCESS THE ABOVE WHILE PREPARING THE DISH

" LOYALTY / DEVOTION "

SPIRALS

A twisted bush,
We catch a look

♥

♥

Souls move by
Two spirits shook

Clothes flower
With tendrils

♥

♥

Limbs brush
Scented skin

♥

Light hazes
Smoke circles

♥

Curving up to
String sounds

♥

Smile entices
Magic delights

♥

Warming hearts
Light unfolding

♥

Bind to depart
Time unwinds

♥

Spiralling hair
Always there

♥

♥

♥

♥

♥

♥

" MYSTERY "

INFINITE CHILLI PESTO PASTA

Packet of Fresh Pasta Spirals

100g Basil

60g Pine Nuts (roasted)

2 Cloves of Garlic

60g Parmesan

170ml/6 floz Olive Oil

Pinch of Ground Black Pepper

Fresh Chilli to taste

A few Basil leaves to decorate.

Put the basil, parmesan, garlic and pine nuts into a food processor and whizz it up. Pour in the oil and whizz again before putting the pesto on a medium heat in a non-stick saucepan to warm through.

Meanwhile, cook the pasta as directed and place into a large bowl. Remove the pesto from the heat and pour over the pasta and mix.

For Alchemical Transformation

"LOYALTY / DEVOTION" resonates to the frequency of number 158; the numerology of which is uplifted through beauty. Can get caught in stubborn insistence, but needs to accept the reality of change.

"MYSTERY" resonates to the frequency of number 175; the numerology of which: Works with the systems beyond human understanding. Rises up to the divine.

PROCESS THE ABOVE WHILE PREPARING THE DISH

" NEW BEGINNINGS "

BACK TO LIFE

At morning sunrise out of bed
Dazed by comfortable sleep
Eyes are open and minds realise
The heavy weight of life

Dressed, conscious away I go
Yet thoughts are somewhat deep
Through the door, down a path
There is no time for strife

Driving, the mind it wanders
To an arduous day ahead
A swarm of bees pass tightly by
Bring thoughts of pollination

Two hundred yards, hares bravely cross
I give way instead
See them safely into a field
Where a deer stands in fixation

Turn right I count the fences
To continue this natural journey
Over a gate pigs cast pink shades
Onto a red-orange sunrise

Through weeping Willow trees that swish
Peacefully for all to see
Slowly by the rippling pond great heron
More winged surprise

Lastly I spot a majestic pheasant
Red, black, purple, white, and brown
The rising sun lights a future
Where nature's presence remains profound

ROASTED MEDITERRANEAN PHEASANT

3 Pheasants

[hung 1 week; plucked, gutted cleaned & halved]

2 Large Long Sweet Red Peppers

2 Red Onions

3 Tablespoons of Olive Oil

50g Sun Dried Tomatoes in Oil

2 Garlic Cloves

1 Tablespoon of Sundried Tomato Paste

1 Teaspoon of Chilli Powder

8 fl/oz Brown Basmati Rice

10 fl/oz Stock (I use Boullion Vegetable Stock)

6floz of Red Wine

6 Ripe Red Plums

2oz Pitted Black Olives

Ground Black Pepper

Preheat oven 180°C / 255° / Gas Mark 4.

Heat the oil in a large saucepan that can also go in the oven. Brown of the game in the oil, remove it from the pan and put to one side for the time being.

Put chopped onions, peppers, sun dried tomatoes, garlic into the same pan and fry. Stir in the rice, sun dried tomato paste and chilli powder.

Next pour in the stock, wine and any remaining seasoning then arrange the game gently on top.

You can then cut the plums in half and put these over the dish and add the black olives before covering the pot with a lid.

Cook for 1 hour and serve with a good dense Rioja.

Serves 6

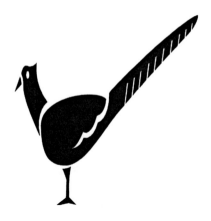

For Alchemical Transformation

"NEW BEGINNINGS" resonates to the frequency of number 180; the numerology of which: Connects to the Inner Teacher. Understands the wealth that is gathered by personal experience

"BLOCKAGE / OBSTRUCTION" resonates to the frequency of number 37; the numerology of which: Brings everything together in order to compute new ideas. Creates abundance or lack, as a reflection of how much fear is held onto by the mind.

PROCESS THE ABOVE WHILE PREPARING THE DISH

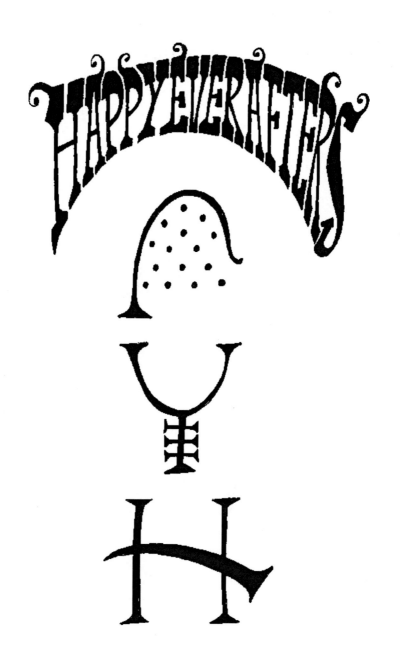

WINTER

AMALGAMATION

PULVERISE

" WILLINGNESS "

THE PEAR

I sat on the tree stump at the side of the clearing pressing my jogging top against my cheekbone. I watched as they threw empty cans of beer at our burning tree. My cheek continued to sting where Bill had lashed at it with a hunk of bark. I didn't care. I loved that tree, and now it was all that was left of her.

As I sat there waiting for them to leave (please leave quickly), I listened to the crackling branches and watched the flames envelope the canopy. Jenny and I came to Winhurst Common all the time. She would come to the shop after her Ballet lesson on a Saturday morning. The paper shop had been in our family for over 70 years and it was my grandfather who employed her. I always thought of him as a quiet wise man.

I was always so happy when Saturday came, she'd arrive on her bike with her long hair flowing and her shoe bag on her back.

"Hi J-Jenny, good to see you, would you like some c-coffee?"

"I'd love some, I've had a whole morning of really tough dance" she smiled, "I brought you all some cake."

Hey, y-you're a star J-Jen. Dad, Jenny's brought us cake. It's from the M-mallories".

I hated my stuttering, these days it only comes very occasionally as I've learnt to control it, back then it was a little more obvious. Strangely though, it only happened with Jenny, when I hadn't seen her for a while. After a couple of minutes in her company it would stop.

Jenny hugged me and I poured out the coffee. Dad arrived, he loved Ella Mallorie's pastries and she had brought him his favourite; Eccles cake.

"Jenny you shouldn't have, but I'm glad you did."

"You're welcome Mr Arnott" she put all the cakes on a plate, not eating herself and I worried for her health. Jenny was obliged to conform to a strict diet to keep her weight down for the ballet.

"Where's your Grandfather Ben? Out in that cactus shed I bet". I nodded as she walked towards the back door with the custard doughnut, leaving me to devour an iced bun.

"She's a good girl Benny boy eh? Your Granddad has an eye for good staff. Will you shelve those magazines while she serves today?"

"Yes Dad, no problem." He winked at me.

"Good on you lad. I'll take this fruit over to your Mother then. Old Stobbart has given me extra oranges for the nurses. He's a soft one eh? See you later."

"B-bye Dad."

The bleeding has stopped now so I put the damp towel away, wondering if chlorine in the blood is dangerous. I should have just walked away instead of trying to defend our precious tree. Instead I'm going to have to explain the bruises to Dad. He'll be in Granddad's shed now, tending to the old cacti as he'd promised the old man he would do when he died. I watched the tree as the flames rose, the sound of the wailing fire-engine sirens alerted Bill and his mates. They were now leaving quickly. I watched while the rush of water dampened out the flames. I felt a physical pain rise in my chest while I took in the result of their crucifixion.

It was easy to remember that afternoon with Jenny. Dad had returned at 3.30pm after seeing Mum. Mum had a rare disease and he never missed her Saturday visit. I also remember he returned a little sooner than usual;

"Do you two want to get off early now? It's a nice day, you should be out in the fresh air Ben - and Jenny you must have practise to do?" He was a thoughtful Father like that.

"Thanks a lot Mr Arnott."

I looked at Jenny's smile, her skin glowed as she stood with her back to the window and the autumn sun streamed through her golden hair.

"Y-yes th-thanks Dad, is there anything you need while I'm out"?

"No. Just make sure you come back in one piece, alright lad?" I knew what he was getting at but he didn't want to embarrass me in front of my first and only love. I stood aside to let Jenny through the door.

"J-Jenny, are you busy this afternoon, I'd really like you to come to the Common with me? It's a lovely afternoon for a walk?"

"Well I, yes of course I would love to Ben, thank you." Jenny was shy, and always a little hesitant. We had walked and talked a lot, she was picked on frequently at her college because she was regarded as a "gifted" dancer by the Royal Academy. Success did not always go down well in the hardened suburbs of working class Manchester. Even so, she was strong-willed and was determined to follow up her love of the Russian Ballet, to embrace her scholarship. I opened the gate at the side of the shop so that she could leave her bike there while we walked. I remember I wanted to hold her hand.

The fireman switched off the hose;

"That's all we can do here Colin, let's get back to the station and fill in the report" "Righto Stan, looks like travellers again. We'll have to do some more visits."

When I was sure they'd gone, I picked up my ruck-sack and walked over to the blackened debris. It was hard to believe we once stood under this tree holding each other for what seemed like light years. I was 19 back then and Jenny was 17. I'm now 30, but it seemed like only yesterday that I held her.

We'd walked towards the common.

"What have you been up to Ben?"

"Quite a lot, I've got good news, they accepted me at Oxford J-Jen! All that speech therapy has paid off.

I'm going to Oxford c-can you believe that? They've accepted me."

"Fantastic, brilliant" she threw her arms around me tightly. I held onto her for perhaps a bit too long. Still, I reasoned in my head we were adults now and she was my friend, my best friend. Anyway, I'd soon be away from her altogether but little did I know then that it would be she who would leave me forever.

We'd reached the Common as the sun blazed through the trees in a hazy afternoon light.

"So where are you taking me" she asked.

"I have to s-show you something, something very special come with me."

I guided her into the woods and to a clearing where in the middle stood the tree.

"That's a lovely tree Ben. Wait though; what's that on the branches? Is it fruit?"

"Go ahead, have a look."

"Pears? Here on the common? How strange, there aren't any other fruit trees here."

"Exactly, I've checked that too, what do you think, the colours are wonderful aren't they? Look the fruit has an almost purple tinge. I mean essentially they're green and red, but look at those lilac shades on the skins".

Without any warning a pear fell from a great height, only missing her head because I leaned forward in time to catch it. Without a thought, I wrapped my arms around her and kissed her. From that day on my stuttering stopped. I thought of Jenny as my tree, a beautiful elegant presence that had saved me from myself.

Recalling that moment I looked up at our tree. The last I heard from Jenny was from Russia where she was dancing her beautiful dream with an established troupe. For me, it was a duty to my family that tied me here. I keep the paper shop running and my education is lost like the time I spent away from her. Stupidly I thought I could live without her because we corresponded regularly during my studies. Then, when she eventually gave up her passport; a result of a disagreement with her parents who were insisting she return to the UK for good, I stopped sending her letters. Sometimes my stutter returns and to rid myself of it, I think of her. Now she dances like a lonely elemental whisper, delicately lighting up the stage with her gentle movements.

I lower myself to the ground, and notice something in the embers something golden and smooth. I pick up the warm metal. Perplexed I regard its golden shape. A golden pear? I look at it bewildered now. What have I got here? I shouldn't have let her go! I lift the object up to the fading sunlight and regard it carefully. My stomach churns over. My eyes sting and a dry metallic taste manifests in my mouth. In one smooth movement the golden pear splits open in my hand!

I look inside and see purple flesh encased in the golden skin! My eyes adjust to an image of her dancing. Her little figure resembles a small fairy against an amethyst background. I blink away the image through the tears. I have to find her! I stand and run. I must bring Jenny back home.

" INTUITION "

PEAR IN CHOCOLATE & CALVADOS SAUCE

4 Ripe Pears (peeled but with the stalks left on)

1 Piece of Root Ginger (peeled and sliced)

5 Cloves

1 Vanilla pod

1 Star Anise

1 Cinnamon Stick

2 Tablespoons of Lemon Juice

750g Raw Cane Sugar

Sauce:

200g Good Quality Dark Chocolate

250ml Double Cream

50ml Calvados

To Serve:

Good Quality Vanilla Ice Cream

Half fill a pan big enough to hold the pears with water (don't put them in yet). Add all the other ingredients and simmer for 10 mins. Drop in the pears and simmer for a further 30 minutes, then take the pears out and set aside.

Break up the chocolate and place in a heatproof bowl. In a separate pan put the cream and calvados, bring to the boil then pour over the chocolate until melted.

Then take each pear by the stalk and dip it into the sauce until completely covered. Remove each pear and place on separate plates.

Add a scoop of Vanilla ice cream and decorate with a stick of cinnamon.

Serves 4.

For Alchemical Transformation
"WILLINGNESS" resonates to the frequency of number 262; the numerology of which: Builds with love. Commits to perfection. Accepts things as they are.
"INTUITION" resonates to the frequency of number 144; the numerology of which: Becomes a 'way-through' for inspirational communication. Teaches others from its own experience.
PROCESS THE ABOVE WHILE PREPARING THE DISH

" HONOURING / RESPECT "

BLIZZARD

Tim woke up at 5am and moved the cat away from his face. At 6 a.m. Mum would be up making him eat breakfast and badgering him to do things for her before school. So he grabbed his brand new exercise book and found a good pen to write with. Miss Juniper insisted they write stories with proper pens which Mum tutted at.

"Full of high and mighty ideas, these younger teachers."

Tim loved his English class and found it hard to persuade Mum to agree to let him go to extra writing sessions on Wednesday nights. It was Wednesday already and he hadn't had a chance to write down any dreams he'd had this week. CS Lewis wrote down his dreams and his books became famous. Miss Juniper told him this when she asked him where his ideas came from. So, it must be true. Moss the cat stood at the bedroom door and meowed;

"Sshhh you impatient ball of fur".

Tim knew he could never ignore Moss, he'd have to feed her soon or she'd wake the whole house and his precious writing time would be gone. He pulled an anorak over his flimsy pyjamas, the house was freezing. Even in winter Mum would not put the heating on and they used a wood burner instead to heat the whole house.

While Moss rubbed around his ankles, he bent to stroke her then spooned out the Felix with some Go Cat. Moss was spoilt but Tim didn't mind and now she was quiet, he was able to pour himself a glass of milk. He sat at the table, taking care not to scrape the chair.

An hour passed before the story was finally finished so at least he had something for Miss Juniper to mark. Hearing the floorboards creak and Mum's bedroom door open, he jumped up and ran the tap at the kitchen sink to start the washing up from the night before.

"You're up early Tim?"

"Homework, I've just done a story about..."

"Good, well come on, finish that washing up. God my head hurts. When you've done that, can you bring some more logs in from the shed?"

"Mum it's snowing outside. Can't we just put the main heating on?"

"Tim, please just go?"

Tim looked at the three empty wine bottles as he placed them in the recycling container. He wondered if three bottles were too much, one day he would drink a bottle and find out for himself.

"Tim, you'll need to take Stephen to the Centre on your way to school, I can't be doing with him today."

Mum pulled at Stephen's arm as he shuffled into the kitchen. She plonked him onto the chair and told him to eat; Stephen was autistic and epileptic and not good at concentrating. For Mum, with her headache, this was too much. She tried to drink her coffee and Tim watched as her small fingers shook.

"Come on Tim, get out there and get those logs in."

"OK Mum, I'm going."

He opened the door to an icy blizzard just as the weather lady had said. After only 5 minutes placing the cold wood into the bucket, his hands felt numb. He ran into the house with the logs and stocked the burner for Mum, who was busy buttoning Stephen's coat. Stephen was fifteen, four years older than him but more like a baby brother. Tim didn't mind this as much as Mum did.

"Right you two, get going now, out of my hair".

The sound of the front door closing behind them was colder than the icy needles of snow prickling at their faces. To reach Stephen's Day Care Centre they had to walk around Fern Oak Big Pond. Tim wondered if things would get any better for Mum now that Dad had left. Stephen talked to himself which was usual and made Tim pity his brother. Although, when he heard the ramblings he felt just a little lonely. It would be good to be able to talk to him properly, anyone actually.

A yelp from Stephen jolted Tim from his thoughts.

"Ouch, hurt!"

Laughs and jeers followed. It was Glyn, the guy from year 11, with his mates.

"Look, here he comes with his weirdo brother" Stephen looked hurt while red anger rose from Tim's throat onto his face. Ignoring them, they walked on but another stone flew at them, this time catching Stephen in the eye. The gang bolted at them from the trees and jumped at Stephen, bringing him to the ground.

"Stop!" Tim grabbed a branch.

"Get off him".

Glyn looked up from his victim, sneered and headed towards Tim, who in a flash of fury, flung the branch at the boy's face. Spots of blood appeared on Glyn's face from the spikes of hawthorn. Seeing the mess now, the others fled. Glyn was left defending himself but, so was Stephen. Having recovered quickly from his attack, he was now kicking and punching his enemy!

"Enough Stephen, it's not worth it."

Tim tried to reason with his brother but he wasn't listening and continued the blows to Glyn's head. Glyn's cries were ignored .

"I said stop Stephen. Leave him!"

Stephen didn't stop. Eventually, Glyn's groans did. The air grew silent and blood poured out, to form a dense crimson carnation in the snow.

"You idiot! Look what you've done." Tears fell from Stephen's wide eyes as Tim turned on him.

"Wasn't me." The tears continued as panic spread across Stephen's face.

"Shut up, idiot." Tim grabbed him by the collar and threw him onto the bench behind them.

"Don't move." Tim's heart pounded at his throat. He stepped backwards and starred at Glyn's still body. Picking up a spiky branch, he prodded at the body. There was no movement - Glyn was dead.

Panicking now, he turned to face Stephen who sat motionless on the bench, his head hanging.
"Get up! Now, over here. Move!" Tim fought the sick rising in his stomach and marched angrily towards his brother.

"Get over here and help me, you retard! Or do you feel like explaining this to the police?" Stephen jumped at the words and headed for the body.

"Now, get down here and push, push him. Hurry up before those idiots come back!"

As the boys put their weight onto the body it rolled laboriously towards the pond. With the last shove, Glyn's corpse plopped heavily into the freezing pond water.

Turning to face his brother now, Tim grasped his head between his hands:

"Right, listen to me. We are going to the Centre now, OK? Nothing happened here this morning. Remember that, OK? Nothing. Repeat it back. Now!"

"Nothing happened." Stephens face was grey with fear as his frightened voice let the syllables fall from his mouth.

The boys walked on in their respective silences while the blizzard continued to thicken. The Big Pond slowly froze over.

" DEPRESSION "

A-MAZING LABRYNTH MUFFINS

1 Large Pear

125ml Vegetable Oil

2 Large Eggs

200g Rice Flour

100g Ground Almonds

175g Raw Cane Sugar

1 Teaspoons Baking Powder

1 Teaspoon Ground Ginger

1 x 142ml Pot of Sour Cream

1 Tablespoon Honey

For Labyrinth Icing

100g Butter

150-200g Icing Sugar

2 Tablespoons Boiling Water

1 Teaspoon Orange Colouring

Preheat oven to 200°C / 392°F / Gas 6 and put 12 muffin
cases in a muffin tin.

Put the flour, baking powder, sugar and ginger into a bowl. Next put the sour cream, oil, honey and eggs into a mixing jug and then fold this mixture into the dry ingredients. Mix in diced pear and then put the mixture into the muffin cases. Cook for 20 mins.

Put the butter in a mixing bowl and whisk until pale and softened. Add 150g of the icing sugar and hot water and whisk again until you get a nice paste.

Add in the food colouring and whisk again. At this point you will be able to see if you need to add any more of the icing sugar.

Put the mixture into a piping bag and pipe on your Labyrinth - this can sometimes be a bit tricky to do.

However, if you can practice, you may well find it a very therapeutic exercise. You can use the Labyrinth at the end of the story if you like or, if you have your own design, please do make use of it.

For Alchemical Transformation

"HONOURING / RESPECT" resonates to the frequency of number 126; the numerology of which is: The inner perfection of the soul as experienced through human relationships. Attitudes and behaviors which reflect the sacredness of life.

"DEPRESSION" resonates to the frequency of number 69; the numerology of which: Makes the choice to go up into the light, or down into the darkness. Gives of the self to inspire others to uplift themselves.

PROCESS THE ABOE WHILE PREPARING THE MUFFINS

" TENDERNESS "

ELEPHANT

To gaze is to see laughter lines
Circle around your small eyes
Sketched in blue, yet you are not
You are just you

Your trunk is thick and
Conceals a tusky smile
You've lived a life heavy
Yet it's a breeze for your tail

With your ears huge and wide
And very far open
You might flap them back
As you raise up your trunk

Your background is warming
In deep sandy beige
From Africa, to a mind
Sketched on a cloth page

I visit you daily on your wall

Strong and sturdy

I know you lift moods

With soft lines of delight

As I turn to leave I cannot resist

A comment on your appearance

"An original" he says indeed it's true

An original Elephant you are

Inspired by a framed sketch on a table cloth, by David Shepherd.

ORACLE OF ORANGE FUDGE

224g Good Quality Plain Chocolate

480g Cups Raw Cane Sugar

2 Tablespoons of Syrup

100ml Cup Single Cream

4 Tablespoons of Butter

3 Tablespoons of Orange Flower Extract

Butter an 8 inch square pan. Melt the chocolate in a pan on a low heat and stir in sugar, syrup and cream. Increase the heat to medium, until the sugar dissolves. Take out any crystals that might have formed in the pan. Increase the temperature to 100°C / 230°C and stir until it reaches the soft ball stage.

Remove from heat and add butter. Let the mixture cool a bit then add orange flower extract and beat the mixture until it begins to thicken. Pour into the 8 inch square pan. Cool the fudge right down then cut into squares to serve.

For Alchemical Transformation
"TENDERNESS" resonates to the frequency of number 253; the numerology of which: Splits the mind down the middle, opens the intellect to the emotions.
"LIMITLESS THINKING" resonates to the frequency of number 154; the numerology of which: Manifests the trinity. Heals with love.
PROCESS THE ABOVE WHILE PREPARING THE SWEETS

MOON

WINE SPIRIT

ESSENCE

" ATTACHMENT "

COMET

Close the carriage door and come
Round here to me my love
Hold my hand and close your eyes, we shall walk
I'll take you into my special night sanctuary

Amongst the vines will we tread without fear
Take off your shoes, press your delicate toes
Down to touch damp ground, trust me as I lead you
To safety don't mind my furnace of a heart

Here, sit on my coat let me lower you so
To place you down on the slope, it was here I first lay
Still and alone scared in my perpetual empty solitude
Gently and slowly lift up your delicate, soft eyelids

Does the sight prickle your skin
As the stars intrinsically ignite you
How you breathe deeply through cold air
As the sky excites you

Now do you see the twinkling explosions wrapping around the soul of our world. Look oh precious one! Feel my touch, so as to catch the approaching Comet

" INTENTION "

WHITE ROSE AND ELDERFLOWER CHAMPAGNE

4 Litres Hot Water

700g Sugar

Juice and Zest of 2 Lemons and 2 Oranges

2 Tablespoons White Wine Vinegar

5 White Rose Flower Heads in Full bloom

10 Elderflower Heads in Full Bloom

Pinch of Dried Yeast (may or may not be needed)

Make sure all equipment is properly cleaned.

Put hot water and sugar into a plastic bucket and stir until the sugar dissolves. Add 2 litres of cold water to top up.

Add orange and lemon juice and zest, vinegar and the flower heads and stir around carefully. Cover with muslin and leave in a cool airy place for 2 days. At this point, take a look to check that the liquid is becoming a bit foamy (beginning to ferment). If not then add the yeast.

Leave mixture to ferment for 4 more days then strain the liquid through a muslin lined sieve into glass bottles; the kind with rubber stopper lids.

Ready to serve after 1 week of bottling.

For Alchemical Transformation
"ATTACHMENT" resonates to the frequency of number 25; the numerology of which: Feels deeply. Takes emotion to extremes in the fight to retain what it knows. Births a consciousness which connects to the highest expression of love.
"INTENTION" resonates to the frequency of number 142; the numerology of which: Uses thought forms to construction Spiritual Will. Manifests truth and wisdom. Lifts the heart into the mind.
PROCESS THE ABOVE WHILE PREPARING THE DRINK

" RESOLUTION / COMMITTMENT "

POPPY WINE - A PLAY

"Eva come in, come in it's been an age since I've seen you."

"My favorite Uncle Alf, hello! Let me hug you; what at journey. I'm so thirsty. Still, thanks to the success of your fabulous wines, I have a lovely new car. Look, do you like it. The roof drops down. It's fantastic in this weather."

"It's great Eva, just great. Put your things there and hurry please, I want to show you something."

"What is it Alf, not more fantastic products, surely."

"Well that's up to you my dear; you're the Marketing Manager. What's that clinking away in your bags?"

"I've brought some bottle samples that I want you to look at; they're 50cls, slightly smaller than the standard size. I thought it would be good to fill them with something classy and aim the wine at the "Ladies that Lunch" market. Have a look, tell me what you think."

"Interesting. Very interesting, my dear."

"I do need some good quality liquid though, a Sauvignon Blanc maybe? I'll need a good duel varietal red and perhaps a Rosé?"

"I see, I see, well you may just have arrived at the right time. Now, this is top secret. We're not going to the intermediaries on this one. It's going to be our profit Eva, 50/50 for you and me. It's what Katti would have wanted for us both."

"Then please let's get on, don't keep me waiting any longer. Lead the way."

"OK, Miss Impatient come with me, we need to take a little walk outside, to the other side of the vines... No, not there dear, I've erected another shed. Here through here, past these vines. Yes that's right, through the arch."

"Oh my goodness Alf look at all these poppies! You've got a whole field of them here and wait, what's that noise? Is it music?"

"It's Rachmaninoff, dramatic eh? They seem to like it."

"Who likes it?"

"The poppies Eva, they love it."

"Are you telling me you're playing Rachmaninoff to a field of poppies?"

"Up there, look I've put up a speaker. It's wired through to the new shed I've built over there."

"That is some shed Alf, it's enormous."

"I switch on the CD, repeat mode, at 4am every day. The music plays all through the growing season, that's each day from dawn right through to dusk and they really do thrive! They absolutely love it girl!"

"How do you know though? That's err, well its madness. Brilliant, but absolute madness!"

"Years now dear, that's how I know. I've kept this field cultivated for 5 years and I've been refining the viticulture and regenerating the seeds each year."

"I had no idea you could be this secretive. Have you really kept all these poppies hidden behind the vines for 5 years? All those visits here and I didn't find it?"

"Yes Eva, you and I have been strolling through these vines for goodness knows how long and every time you visit I've walked you right past that honeysuckle arch! Ha ha! A smart secret I've kept from you eh?"

"That's crazy Alf! I do love you, you are so eccentric. There is no doubt about it you are simply the most important and most special person I know."

"Well come on, let's go to the shed, you haven't seen the best of it yet."

"My goodness, just look at all this equipment! The place is like an inventor's shrine! How many vats and demi-johns do you have here producing this stuff?"

"I know, I know Eva, it's in hand, I've finally come round to your way of thinking and ordered some proper tanks. We take delivery this Friday. You are a clever girl I couldn't do this without your commercial knowledge. "Here take this glass and sit yourself down, you'll need to be comfortable to try this stuff".

"So, when will the liquid be ready Uncle Alf?"

"As soon as you can get those classy new bottles delivered. It's just a call to Chris and he'll have the liquid bottled up quicker than you can get the orders in. You'll need to get your label people onto it right away, and the dispatch organized. I don't have the environment to stack cases and bottles.

Anyway, enough of this poppy-cock (pardon the pun). What about the colour Eva?"

"Alf it's incredible. How did you get it to this shade? I mean Rosé doesn't usually have a lilac tinge? People are going to be very inquisitive about this one".

"It's the seeds dear. The petals are giving it the Rosé its colour, and the seeds send through that fabulous lilac glow."

"How on earth did you think of this?"

"Ah my beautiful niece, you would not believe me if I told you."

"Please, do try me Alf because even if I don't believe you, I do need to get this past the vultures at the hygiene test centre."

"Yes, err, well…"

"You're hiding something Alf?"

"OK, OK. It was a dream."

"A dream?"

"Yes yes! A dream, the formula came to me in a dream."

"What do you mean?"

"It was Katti, Aunt Katti spoke to me in my sleep!"

"Aunt Katti spoke to you in a dream? Darling Alf, you know you should call me if you feel lonely. I'll come, you know that. Don't let these night worries get the better of you now."

"I know Eva but listen that's not the point. I planted the field of poppies for her and then I was thinking of selling off that land. I've had some good offers but then she spoke to me in this dream, 5 years ago."

"5 years is a long time, honestly you must have adored her."

"Now stop it please, these are details that aren't relevant at the moment. Will you not taste my wine?"

"But what did she say to you in the dream?"

"Must you continue to go on with this?"

"I must."

"Well she gave me the formula that's all."

"And.."

"And she told me not to sell the land where the poppies grow, simple. There you have it, it started there and I began production. Come Eva, I'm excited and getting tired all at the same time. We must to have dinner soon and I need to know what you think. Go on now, smell it".

"OK, I'm getting flowers on the nose, yet it's very delicate and, well just a very light scent".

"Yes yes, that's the easy part, what else?"

"Well, I think it's the seeds! I can smell the seeds and a narcotic spice. No wait, not spices, more of a herby sweetness."

"Excellent it's done. Success at last! Great Eva, that's exactly what I wanted you to smell"? Taste it now. Go on, I dare you to taste it".

"What on earth...! It's heaven, I've never tasted anything so delicate and so clear on the palate too. But wait. What's this after taste, this length I'm getting? It's so unusual and unexpected. Its hmmmm..."

"Hmmmm indeed, that's the seeds, I've had to work so hard on refining them. I've got it down to a fine art, a secret fine art mind you. Keep it between us now - it's 4 parts petals to 1 part seeds and a few Grenache grapes. We can still call it wine for the market, do you see?"

"Uncle Alf what have you done here, what has happened during the vinification process? I err, well I feel great, and I'm not drunk. You know..?"

"Yes I know dear, fantastic isn't it? What wine does that, makes it possible for you access those senses to such a depth?"

"Yes, I just feel extremely relaxed and happy. Everything is so acute and bright and I am so, oh so peaceful..."

"There you have it dear, that's the ingredients working their magic. It's no £4.99 Rosé is it? Pretty special stuff if you ask me Eva, and don't you be concerned, the liquid is not as potent as it feels. It's important that one sticks to a few glasses sure, which is why I think your bottles are ideal. We must be careful how much we sell at a time that's all."

"It is unbelievably intoxicating, and beautiful; the colour, the scent, well everything! Do you really want me to sell this? I mean, well you know, I sense some of Katti's old magic at work here. You know that too don't you Alf? Could it not be a bit, well you know, perhaps a little dangerous."

"Maybe yes, in the wrong hands, but we must put this out to market now. We'll license it somehow Eva because people are really going to be ready for this kind of liquid. It's very sophisticated and besides, it's Katti's legacy to us."

"Thank you Uncle Alf, you're right. We can't let her down and I've never experienced anything so exquisite. Let's set a date for production".

"Right away dear."

" SPIRITUALITY / RECOGNISING OWN DIVINITY "

POPPY WINE

12 Poppy Petals (if this is tricky use Rose Petals)

2 Bottles of Sauvignon Blanc

250ml Crème de Cassis

Packet of Poppy Seeds

12 Lemon Balm Leaves

You will need:

12 x 175ml Wine Glasses

Separate 250ml Bottle with Rubber Stopper

Swizzle Stick

Ice Cube Tray – 12 Section (any shape you like)

Night Before

On the night before you wish to serve your poppy wine, put the 2 bottles of Sauvignon Blanc in the fridge. Take some of the poppy seeds from the bag and keep them aside for the ice cubes.

Fill an ice cube tray with water and add 1 poppy petal to each cube together with a pinch of whole poppy seeds. Place the 12 cube ice tray into the freezer.

Then pour 250ml Crème de Cassis into a tall glass bottle with a rubber stopper. In a pestle and mortar grind the remaining poppy seeds as finely as you can and put these into the bottle with the Crème de Cassis.

On the night

Open the wine bottles and pour the 125ml of the Sauvignon Blanc into the 175ml glasses. You can then add as much of the Crème de Cassis (it may need agitating a little) to taste without any fear of spillage. Remember you will also need to add ice cubes.

Add a poppy petal and seed ice cube to each glass and use a swizzle stick to mix. Finally, finish off by topping each wine glass with a lemon balm leaf. Makes 12 glasses.

For Alchemical Transformation

"RESOLUTION / COMMITTMENT" resonates to the frequency of number 205; the numerology of which: Makes up its mind to be steady. Focuses through the levels of emotion to the clarity beyond. Is aware of choice.

"SPIRITUALITY / RECOGNISING OWN DIVINITY" resonates to the frequency of number 241; the numerology of which cuts through matter with great sensitivity. Synthesises love and trust

PROCESS THE ABOVE WHILE PREPARING THE WINE

" COURAGE / ENCOURAGEMENT "

HAPPY BIRTHDAY

This is just a note to say
In of course, the very best way

A very Happy Birthday to you
From a friend who's heart is good and true

Eat some cake, drink some wine
And I'm sure your day will be very fine

Then when your day is finally done
Take yourself home and have lots of fun

I wish you peace as you turn off the light
Your birthday star, shines long and bright

" VISION / VISIONARY "

DREAM INDUCING HOT CHOCOLATE

1oz Grated Belgian Milk Chocolate

1oz Grated Dark Chilli Chocolate

¼ Teaspoon of Vanilla Extract

¾ Cup of Milk

¼ Cup Thick Cream

For an Optional Topping

Can of Squirty Cream

Some Ground Cinnamon, Cocoa Powder or

Chopped Nuts

Put the milk, milk chocolate, chilli chocolate and vanilla extract into a saucepan and cook over a low heat (do not boil). Stir gently until the milk warms through and melts the chocolate completely. Add the thick cream and cook for a further 1-2 minutes i.e. until warm before pouring the mixture into a mug.

Topping:

Squirt on a cream spiral topping and sprinkle with Cinnamon, Cocoa Powder or chopped nuts.

For Alchemical Transformation
"COURAGE / ENCOURAGEMENT" resonates to the frequency of number 63; the numerology of which: Rises about the constraints of the mind. Completes a cycle of actions.
"VISION / VISIONARY" resonates to the frequency of number 260; the numerology of which: Sees the opportunities for pro-creation. Surrenders to the process to make it happen.
PROCESS THE ABOVE WHILE PREPARING THE DRINK

TARRADIDDLE

IS WRITTEN WITH UNCONDITIONAL LOVE

IN CONSIDERATION OF EARTH, WIND, FIRE, WATER AND AIR

FOR ALCHEMICAL TRANSFORMATION AND COMPLETION

ACKNOWLEDGEMENTS

I would like to say a very big THANK YOU to the following people for their kindness and support. Without the help of these special people (be it in a small or large way, and consciously or not) Tarradiddle would not have emerged:-

Alison & Stephen Bishop
Helen Brown
Ceri MacLeod
Wellington & Reuben Evans
Susie & Howard Gibbons
Gladstone Henry
Sian Kleeman
David Lawson
Tracy MacKenzie & Family
Nick Munday
Katie Ruff
Barry Spenceley & Family
Carol Vernon
Jackie Wilson

Ruth Brecher
Richard Bernard
Tom & Louise Evans*
Sonja Galsworthy
Maxi & Cyril Harvey
Kath Higgens
Kay Kraty*
Stacy McEvoy
David Maskrey
Neil Perry
Mr Smokey
Peter Tuckey
Effie & Peter Vincent
Lisa & Ellie Wilson

Tom Evans: Metaphysics & www.tomevans.co/witwtm/
Kay Kraty: Life Symbols and their meaning Kaykraty@aol.com
Ian Ludlow: Life Symbol Images ijstudio@btconnect.com
David Maskrey - Internal Section Drawings
Stacy McEvoy - Graphics Coordinator
www.visualthesaurus.com & www.canstockphoto.com

TARRADIDDLE

Offbeat Tales and Alchemical Eats

"In her debut presentation of tales, verses and magical repas, Wendy Spenceley delivers an alchemical mix to tantalise the taste buds and nourish your literary appetite"

"Just when you think the market can't produce another cookery book, this Author / Practitioner from Surrey delivers a scintillating read and some delightful eats

– A new and transformational way to entertain –"

In this debut volume: Tarradiddle - Offbeat Tales and Alchemical Eats, the author dazzles us with alchemical surprises.

.

- A daring and ambitious first book - "

ABOUT THE AUTHOR

Wendy Spenceley has been living and working in Surrey for some 20 years and originally pursued a degree in Business Studies at Kingston University.

After a change of direction she then went on to practice Alchemical Aromatherapy and more recently, worked with crystals and all types of symbols in a transformational way. Wendy then found a different level of enlightenment that gave her the ability to find a strong and peaceful strength. She then found it possible to pass on this knowledge to people around her and enable them to find a positive direction in all that they do.

After this period of enlightenment the writer attended a class in creative writing. Wendy then found her way to an event in Guildford where she met Tom Evans; an author mentor and published author himself. Tom assisted her to tap into ways of manifesting her writing dreams and bring her books into the public domain.

More recently, Wendy has been writing more stories and poems that provide a platform for her transformational energy to develop. This adventure has lead to the creation of some interesting Alchemical recipes. To add to the transformational element of this work, Wendy selected and traced symbols over her recipes and writing and this added an informative and progressive energy to her creations. This became a deeply enhancing experience in many ways.

If you would like to know more about Wendy please follow and send any questions via her blog offbeattales.wordpress.com